The Murders of Molly Southbourne

T0383038

ALSO BY TADE THOMPSON

Rosewater
Gnaw
Making Wolf

THE MURDERS OF
MOLLY SOUTHBOURNE

TADE THOMPSON

A TOM DOHERTY ASSOCIATES BOOK

NEW YORK

This is a work of fiction. All of the characters, organizations, and events portrayed in this novella are either products of the author's imagination or are used fictitiously.

THE MURDERS OF MOLLY SOUTHBOURNE

Copyright © 2017 by Tade Thompson

All rights reserved.

Cover photograph © Rekha Garton/Arcangel
Cover design by Christine Foltzer

Edited by Carl Engle-Laird

A Tor.com Book
Published by Tom Doherty Associates
175 Fifth Avenue
New York, NY 10010

www.tor.com

Tor® is a registered trademark of
Macmillan Publishing Group, LLC.

ISBN 978-0-7653-9712-6 (ebook)
ISBN 978-0-7653-9713-3 (trade paperback)

First Edition: October 2017

For Hunter,
Pectus est quod disertos facit.

Acknowledgments

I keep telling myself I should write this simultaneously with the book to reduce the risk of leaving someone out. Ah, well. Many people helped me with this book in major and minor ways. Thanks to Aliette de Bodard, Zen Cho, Fran Wilde, Stephanie Saulter, J. Courtenay Grimwood, Elizabeth Bear, Kaaron Warren, Cassandra Khaw, Stephen Graham Jones, Nick Wood, Wole Talabi, Chikodili Emelumadu.

For the Russian perspective, Drs. Dilyara Todd and Galina Zhinchin. For transcendent editing, Carl Engle-Laird.

With each failure, each insult, each wound to the psyche, we are created anew. This new self is who we must battle each day or face extinction of the spirit.

Writings on the Natural History of the Mind
Theophilus Roshodan, 1789

The Murders of Molly Southbourne

One

I wake into a universe defined by pain.

I can only open my eyes to slits, and the lids are so swollen, it feels like staring out of a hamburger. Warm fluid trickles out of my nose, but that doesn't worry me as much as the warm pool I appear to be lying and sliding around in. Every part of my body hurts. It hurts to breathe, it hurts to hold my breath, it hurts to think. The fabric I'm wearing hurts against my skin. I close my eyes to rest the lids, then I open them again because I have no idea where I am.

I am in shackles. There are cuts on my ankles and my wrists. I'm in a room somewhere, dim, cold air, wet with my own warm piss. I do not think any of my bones are broken, but I don't want to take a chance. I stay as still as possible, breathing shallow, careful. Careful. My chains link up to rings embedded in the wall, a foot off the ground, forcing me into an awkward position with most of my lower torso flat, but my shoulders and head off the ground. The cement work is shoddy, as if someone did the job without the necessary expertise. It is an old chain with rust in the shape of spilled liquid, like blood. Mine? Other prisoners'? I don't know which is worse.

I know things, but I can't remember them. I feel teased by them. Have I had a head injury? It's odd remembering that a head injury can cause memory loss but not remembering my phone number or my mother's name or if I like coffee black. It's like knowing someone is beside you, but not being able to turn your head.

The walls are plastered, but painted on only three sides. I am facing a door, which is unvarnished wood. There is a second door on the other side of the room, same wall. The whole room seems to have been abandoned midway through decoration. The ceiling is concrete, which suggests there are floors above me. Or maybe not. Maybe I'm in a bunker.

I lose time, or time passes. There is no clock, and the sameness makes time seem static, but my nose stops bleeding and the pulse I hear in my ears slows. My eyelids are less swollen. I hear a key in the lock, and the door opens. A woman comes in, maybe in her twenties or early thirties, long dark hair, athletic, casually dressed, face bruised. She has a carrier bag in her left hand. For the brief period that the door is open, I hear knocking, as if some insistent person is at another door.

"Are you calm?" she asks. "Have you calmed down?"

I try to talk. My throat is too dry, and the sound that

comes out is close to a death rattle. I wonder if I have ever seen anyone die, in this life that I can't remember. I close my mouth again, no point.

"If you attack me I will drive my elbow into your voice box. I know how to do this, and you will most likely die. Are you calm?"

I nod, discovering a pain in my neck. I stop moving.

She leaves the bag near the door and approaches, manhandling me into a sitting position. Up close, I see that her eyes are blue-grey, and that she must be very strong considering the ease with which she shifts me. She smells of peppermint, and there is dirt under her fingernails, blood on her knuckles. I wonder if her injuries match the ones on me. She returns to the door, retrieves the bag, and kneels in front of me. Water from a plastic bottle. I drink and it feels like a balm down my throat. She feeds me small strips of chicken and clumps of bread. I swallow with difficulty, but eagerly.

"Thank you," I say.

She stops, sucks her teeth, packs up the food, and leaves.

～

She returns after a few hours, or some days. It is hard to tell. She has a needle and a bottle of black ink. She comes to me, rolls up my sleeve, and, using a lighter, heats the end of the needle. She applies the heated point and the ink to my skin. I break out in a sweat, but am determined not to cry out. She is very meticulous in writing the tattoo. It is a series of numbers, and it appears she is more concerned with legibility than aesthetics. This takes a long time, and I do not think she is experienced. Given the number of times she swears, I think this may be her first time.

When she finishes, she says, "Keep it clean and dry."

"I am lying in my own urine and feces. How am I meant to keep it clean? Why am I here?"

The woman does not respond, but she seems to slow in her stride before slamming the door shut.

~

Sometime later, at night maybe, the woman bursts into the room, snapping me out of a doze. She is completely naked and unshod. I worry that this is a strange sex ritual, or kidnapping for profit by gangsters, but she seems surprised to see me and there are no cameras. Her face betrays bemusement.

"Oh," she says, then she walks out again, leaving the door ajar. She peeps back, eyes more focused, checking on me, after which she does not return. I hear noises, then the door shuts and the lock turns.

What the hell is going on?

～

The woman comes in again, fully clothed in short sleeves, jeans, tennis shoes. This time she has a chair in tow, wooden, functional, no finish. She locks the door behind her. She also has a pile of rags, a glass of water, a first aid box, a can of lighter fluid, and a gleaming kitchen knife. She lays these items out in a curve in front of her, again making me imagine cultish rituals. She makes eye contact, then picks up the knife. She draws the knife along her forearm. It bleeds brisk red drops, which she aims into the rags. When the flow falters she dresses the wound. She pours the lighter fluid on the floor, creating a wick that flows outside the room. She packs the rags up and takes them out of the room, then comes back in, sits in the chair, and looks at me again.

"My name is Molly Southbourne."

She says this like it should mean something.

"I don't know you," I say, but it rings false, even to me. "Please let me go."

"It's all right. You will know me. You will." She nods to herself. "I'm going to tell you a story. It's long, but you must try to remember it. Your life depends on how well you remember. Will you promise to remember?"

"I—"

"Just promise." No mercy in those eyes. No evil either, just finality, which is scarier.

"I promise."

"Good. Afterwards, I will release you."

Death can be a release, I think, but I don't push the matter. I think she is mad. I feel I should be more afraid, but I am not. I don't know why.

She sighs. "I don't even know where to start. What should I . . ." She seems to be pleading with me.

I hold her gaze the way I would a rabid dog's. When I don't look away, she says, "My earliest memory was a dream. . . ."

Two

Molly's first memory is of her father killing her. At the time, she thinks it is a dream. She sees her father in her room hitting her and she is on the floor with no clothes on. He keeps hitting until she stops moving, then Molly screams. It is as if she is both on the floor, bleeding and dying, and on the bed, watching her father breathing heavily, hands red. Molly struggles to get out of her mother's grip. Her mother tells her she has had a nightmare. Her mother says the bad dream is because she lost a tooth that day. Molly tongues the gap in the front row of her teeth. Her mother sings a song from the old country, and Molly soon falls asleep. When she wakes up the next morning she immediately examines the carpeting, but there is nothing. It seems cleaner than it was, but otherwise it is the same. It will be years before she realizes that this really happened.

∼

Age five, Molly has the run of Southbourne Farm. She is

happy and knows all the animals by name—the names she has given them, at any rate. There are sheep, three horses, two dogs, chickens. She names them all, like a modern-day Eve. Many times she feels so alone, like she is the only one alive, the first and last human. She never leaves the farm. She sits under the largest tree and stares at the world beyond the gate. There are people out there, grown ones like Ma and Pa, little ones like Molly. She has seen them on television. There is also Trevor, who collects the milk, and Erin, who brings the post. They like Molly and bring her things from the outside, little toys and hard candy and homemade boiled sweets. Pile, the German shepherd, plops down next to her. He is old now. Pa says he is twelve, which is old for a dog. Molly loves Pile.

Her father's combine harvester breaks the quiet of the morning. Her mother would be working numbers into columns that Molly did not understand. It is a hot day, and Molly dozes. She falls asleep and puts sudden weight against Pile's forepaw and he bites her, drawing blood. Molly screams. Her mother comes and shoos away the dog, who looks confused. Pa does not hear the scream over the engine. Ma dresses Molly's wound, but Pa takes his shotgun and leaves the house. Molly never sees Pile again. She misses him.

Two days later there is a little girl under the tree.

The farmland slopes gently toward the house, after which it descends again. Because of this, you can see the whole farm from the top floor, or the roof. Molly is on the second floor, and sees the girl from her window. The girl is in shadow, and not wearing any clothes. Molly squeals with surprise. She runs to her wardrobe and selects a dress, then flies out to the tree. She stops short when the girl turns to her. She looks exactly like Molly. It's like seeing herself in the mirror after Ma bathes her. Molly checks where Pile bit her, but the girl does not have the same wound.

"Hello," says Molly.

The girl breaks into a smile, and Molly decides she likes her. She offers the dress, and the girl puts it on.

"Who are you?" asks Molly.

There is a brief crease on the girl's brow, then she says, "Molly."

"Me too!"

For three days they live together in Molly's room. She splits her food in half and takes it upstairs, where the other Molly eats it. They play with Molly's toys and read her picture books as well as they can. She sleeps under the bed until Ma has gone, then they squish together under the covers.

They are playing by the tiny stream that seals the northern boundary of Southbourne Farm when the new girl stops smiling. Molly splashes her with water to try to get her to smile. The girl snatches up a rock and swings it at Molly, cracking her on the head. Molly screams, feels blood stream down the side of her head. She pushes at the girl ineffectually. She calls for her mother. The girl keeps hitting her with the rock.

Molly's eyes close. She hears someone say, "Hey!" then an explosion that seems to come from far away. She opens her eyes briefly, only to see her mother standing there with a smoking handgun. Molly falls away and reemerges in her own bed.

"She's awake," says an unfamiliar voice. Her head feels tight. A woman in a nurse's uniform comes into view.

"Hello there, Molly. How are we feeling? You took a nasty spill."

"Where's Molly?" asks Molly. She does not recognize her own voice. It sounds thick.

"*You're* Molly, darling."

"I know that. Where's the other Molly?"

"I'm Alana, your nurse. I think you're confused."

Molly isn't confused, but she knows grown-ups. At times they say things that are not true, and what they want is for you to agree with them. They especially like it when you nod.

Molly nods and says, "I'm confused."

Alana smiles. "I'll go get your parents."

A doctor comes in to check on Molly. While he examines her he notices the tulips on the windowsill. He says that in Japan there is a custom of bringing potted plants to sick people instead of flowers, because flowers are dead or dying. Molly is unsure if this story is meant to be funny or comforting, so she smiles. Adults like that. The doctor tells her parents that he wants to take Molly in for a scan, but they refuse.

At night, Molly sometimes hears gunshots, and she has dreams, nightmares about the other Molly, but these fade with time.

They never talk about it, but Molly's life changes. There are rules now. More rules than before, and stranger than eating with her mouth closed or keeping her elbows off the dining table.

"If you ever see a girl who looks like you, run. If you can't run, fight. Your mother or I will take care of it as soon as we get there. But you run and you scream. Do you understand?"

"If I see another Molly, I run, scream, and fight."

"Yes."

"Daddy?"

"What?"

"I don't know how to fight."

"We will fix that."

~

To run or fight is the most important rule, but there is also the blood rule. *Don't bleed.* What that means is *Be careful.* No climbing trees, no running on concrete, no more playing with dogs. No shag rugs. The corridors and rooms are cleared of obstructions. No operating machinery. Soft toys. Good lighting everywhere. Most furniture with curved edges. Good shoes, heels checked every week for wear and replaced promptly.

If you do bleed, blot it all up and burn it. Go back to the spot and flood it with bleach.

"If you ever find a pit or a hole in the ground or in the trees or walls in the house, find me or your mom immediately."

~

The rules are simple.

If you see a girl who looks like you, run and fight.

Don't bleed.

If you bleed, blot, burn, and bleach.

If you find a hole, find your parents.

Molly recites the lines to herself many times. She finds herself repeating them without intending to when she is bored.

She learns about the different types of bleach, and how to make a flame from the simplest of materials, focusing on what burns hottest, not necessarily brightest.

"It's a mistake to go for the spectacular flames, Molly," her mother tells her. "Pyromaniac arsonists want spectacle, because they want the flame. We want the destruction. The hottest, most destructive flame is invisible. Visible flames are caused by incomplete combustion."

Her mother knows a lot about fire.

~

Molly loves music, but all efforts at teaching her to play an instrument fail. She has an interest in listening, but no inclination to compose or create. There are enough musicians in the world, and uncountable hours of compositions; why should she add to this? Sometimes she imagines all the music in the world, since the dawn of time, playing at the same time in a magnificent cacophony, from the first primates who beat out sounds with sticks to the most exquisite Stravinsky. She thinks at the end of time there will be nuclear symphonies played out as radio signals bouncing around on immortal satellites sent out to an uncaring universe.

Her preferences run to Chopin and Fela Kuti, although the latter is one of her mother's favorites, rather than something Molly picks up herself.

"Listen to the words, *dorogoy*. In Fela's words you can divine the nature of intelligent discourse. Notice how he defines *suegbe,* then he defines *pako*. He defines terms, then he explains his thesis. Go forth and do likewise."

Molly listens. The song is called "Suegbe na Pako." She thinks Fela defines with examples. An example has aspects of a thing, but is that the thing itself? The mollys have aspects of Molly, but that doesn't make them Molly, does it?

She does not tell her mother this, because adults like to be right all the time.

~

Molly is nine.

She and her father are in the barn. The air is full of blood and the smell of offal. Her father is holding a knife and a cleaver. There is a dead pig on a slab. An old pig, dead from some illness that gave it seizures. For Molly, a lesson.

"Make sure your tools are sharp and clean. Sharpen them after a single use."

"Can I sharpen them now?"

"No. You're not touching knives yet."

He prepares the skin with boiling water. "This pig died without trauma, so we won't get a lot of blood. It's congealed within the veins and arteries and trapped in the muscles. First thing you want to do is cut the head off. Cut between the vertebrae, do not saw. This is normally a two-man job."

"Two-person," says Molly.

"Two-person." Her father smiles. "But when you're going to need to do this, you'll be alone. You don't need a second person, but it makes the work easier. We . . . you will not have any tools except knives. Once you've separated the head, take off the upper limbs. Do not hack through bone. Divide the cartilage at the joints. Slice through the skin and feel for the line of cleavage."

With a few well-aimed strokes the pig's forelimbs seem to fall off. "Same thing for the lower limbs."

A fly buzzes in and Molly chases it out. There is more blood than she expects. The pig is now a lump of meat. Her father cuts a line across the front of its belly and digs about in the wound. He widens the line down both sides under the rib cage, like a gigantic smile.

"The chest and belly are like a tube of flesh and bone. What you want to do is remove the organs in one piece so you don't make a mess." He reaches into the wound and pulls, emerges with the gullet in his hand, which he ties into a simple overhand knot. Then he reaches into the lower half and ties up the large intestine. Finally he lifts out the entire digestive system, which he plops into a bucket.

"From here on in, it's easy. No blood, no shit."

Molly giggles. "You said 'shit.'"

He winks at her. "Let's not tell Mommy.

"So now you have seven pieces and one bucket of viscera. No sharp edges because you haven't chopped any bone, meaning you can dispose of the whole thing using polyethylene bags." He stands with his arms spread out by his sides. "Did you get all that?"

Molly nods.

"Right. Let's go over it again."

~

At night Molly sees monsters sometimes. She no longer gets scared because it has been going on since as long as she can remember. She sees them only at night, hiding in the bushes. They have long black bodies and eyes that sometimes glint, although sometimes they have no eyes at all. Her father told her that they are just bushes shaped like monsters. Her mother taught her a word for it: pareidolia. It is true that in the daytime she does not see them, but what Molly does is she stands at her window at night and draws the outline of the monster she sees each night. Come daylight she compares the night shape against the shape of the grass or trees or bushes. They do not match. On a windy night when all the bushes are leaning westward, the monster moves *east*. It moves against the wind, and cannot be grass. But she stops telling her parents, because adults usually like you to agree with them, especially when they say you are being silly. Besides, the monsters have never harmed her, or even spoken to her.

In the day she runs through the house like an explorer, trying to find the monsters but instead coming across odd bits and bobs. A Corona typewriter with a severed ribbon and several keys missing. Sheaves of typewritten documents. A play called *The Wisdom of Dead Clowns*, no author.

```
FADE IN:
INT.—DAY
    Inside Sean's flat. A shot of Sean. He is dead
with a spatter pattern on the wallpaper behind his
head. His eyes are open. Some blood dribbles out
of the left angle of his mouth.
    Leigh comes into the shot, still holding the
smoking gun. She flops down beside Sean and picks
up his journal.
    She opens a random page.
    Leigh (reading)
```

"WHAT IS THERE TO LOVE BUT TIGHT FRIENDSHIP AND
A BIT OF FUCKING?"

(turns to Sean's corpse)

YOU ARE REALLY DAMAGED, MY FRIEND. I MEAN . . .
BESIDES THE OBVIOUS, OF COURSE. I'LL BET YOU
WEREN'T BREAST-FED.

She kisses him on the mouth, tongue around
his, licking up the blood, breathing heavy as if
aroused. When this is over her mouth is smeared
with his blood. She picks up the pen and opens the
journal to the last page.

She begins to giggle and write.

FADE OUT.

Molly does not understand or like it, but she finishes
reading. She picks up another one, which lacks a title. It
seems to be about a man with a strange portal in his belly.
Aliens come out of it, killing him in the process of cutting their way out. Molly stops reading. There are other
plays and screenplays, but she feels they are too grue-
some or bizarre to be interesting. She whacks the keys of
the Corona a few times, then she skips out.

～

Molly and her mother go for spas sometimes, to pam-
per themselves. Molly does not understand why they

have to lie facedown in their birthday suits with warm stones on their backs, or spend *hours* in scented water. Her mother buries her under bubbles and says one day she will understand. The massage hurts, and Molly thinks of retaliating, but she feels her mother would frown on it. She retaliates in her mind. She will pick the index finger of the masseuse and bend it back till it hurts, then snaps. While she is bent over in agony, Molly will knee her in the nose. It would take less than a minute.

"I love you, Molly," says her mother.

She knows adults usually want to hear the same words back. Instead she turns to her mother and asks, "What is there to love but tight friendship and a little fucking?"

Her mother and the masseuse both gasp, and Molly realizes she has said the Wrong Thing. Her mother speaks in a language Molly does not understand and frowns. She does that sometimes, lapses into a language that nobody else speaks. They complete the spa in silence.

A few days later, when Molly goes back into the room where the typewriter is, there are no plays in sight.

∼

Five years pass before Molly sees another girl who looks like her, another molly.

One day blood starts to come out from between her legs. She has not hurt herself, she has been careful. If anything, she's been safer than ever. She has been spending a lot of time in bed—headache and belly cramps.

Don't bleed.

She feels shame and fear. She blots at the blood, but it keeps coming. She cannot tell her parents; they will think she has been bad.

Don't bleed.

By the end of the first day she has a bundle of sheets and towels, not soaked, but smeared with blood. She has a hand-towel bundled in her underwear and she pretends to be sick. At night she creeps out and buries the bloodstained linen. The bleeding flows all night, seeping, continuous, fueling her fear. She locks her door, falls asleep, wakes up with her bedsheet soaked through. There is a knock at the door. She thinks it is her parents, but it is a molly. Molly has forgotten the one from before like a bad dream. It is a shock to see herself outside herself. She forgets to run.

"Let me in," says the molly.

Run.

Fight.

Molly lets the molly in. She is torn. She has to tell her parents, but she doesn't want to get in trouble. The molly seems docile and sits calmly on the bed, and Molly can't help noticing that there is no blood between those thighs.

"Put some clothes on," says Molly.

The molly knows where the clothes are, and exactly what to wear. They all fit perfectly, of course.

Run.

The molly stares with grey eyes, unblinking.

Fight.

"Do you know Systema too?"

"Yes."

Molly knows this is not a twin, and that she is in danger, or will be, but the molly looks just like her. It will be like fighting herself. And the bleeding is just too much, she has to tell Ma.

Run.

Fight.

Blot, burn, bleach.

Molly first goes to where she buried the linen. There are five holes. Two mollys stand there, skin forming gooseflesh in the breeze.

Find your parents.

Now she runs. The two mollys follow her, slowly at first, but then with the same speed.

"Mother!"

Molly closes doors behind her, but she can hear the

mollys opening them. They know what she knows. Her mother appears at the top of the stairs.

"Molly?"

"They're coming," says Molly. She does not have to say who.

Mother steps aside for Molly to pass and yells, "Connor!"

Molly hears banging from another part of the house, the other molly trying to get out of her room.

Her mother shoves her into her parents' room and locks her in. Molly sits on the bed and listens to the sounds of conflict. No words, just smacking noises, feet on stairs and floorboards, exhalations, silence.

Molly feels waves of hot and cold come over her and she cannot sit still.

"Ma?"

"Stay where you are, Molly. Just don't come out."

"Listen to your mother," says her father.

He sounds like he is crying. Later Molly smells a barbecue, but she knows it is the mollys burning.

~

Molly bleeds every month. Her mother says it is normal, all women do this.

"Why?" asks Molly.

"*Slezy razocharovannoy matki.* Tears of a disappointed womb."

"What does that mean?"

"It means you are a woman now. You can have children of your own if you aren't careful." Ma seems uncomfortable.

Molly is silent for a while, thinking. "You mean, like the mollys?"

Her mother seems stricken. "No, *dorogoy*. Not like the mollys." She squeezes Molly tight, and in adult-talk, this means don't ask any more questions. So she doesn't.

~

Two years later, Molly still recites the rules to herself.

If you see yourself, run.

Don't bleed.

Blot, burn, bleach.

Find a hole, find your parents.

She knows the rules and does not need to recite them, but they have a talismanic quality now.

She can do a hundred push-ups. She can run very fast, and she can make her way to any part of the house blindfolded. She knows how to disable or kill an opponent in three moves, but she has never killed a molly. She thinks her father does the bulk of the . . . disposal, but her mother has had to from time to time.

Her mother teaches her Systema and her father teaches her how to shoot. She is a middling marksman. She has a room full of books that her mother sends away for. Molly loves reading. Words used to be homework, a chore, but books make words do magic tricks. She loves that writers make words their servants and bend them to their will. She loves the poets, Blake and Shakespeare most of all.

Prisons are built with stones of Law. Blake. Molly thinks she's in a prison of her rules.

She realizes she is partly multilingual, because her mother's words are mixed with Russian, Ukrainian, and some exotic others that even she does not remember.

"My work took me places," Mykhaila says when Molly asks. She does not say what kind of work, but Molly surmises that it involved breaking an attacker's little finger by bending it backward sharply, then kicking the person in the crotch.

The mollys grow as Molly does. Each one is her size and shape, although they do not have her scars. Their hair is wilder, as if it has not been cut, but it is the same pitch-black as Molly's. They have grey-blue eyes that start out bland, but end steely with rage. Molly does not understand this. Why are they angry? Why do they go bad? They always go bad. Always. Usually within three days, but sometimes at shorter intervals. Molly has also noticed that the mollys' blood does not grow other mollys. Like sterile drones. Do they have monthlies?

The smell of burning leaves comes through her open window, likely from another farm. Molly cannot see the smoke, but at least she knows it's not from burning dead mollys.

Some people come from the Social to ask about Molly's education. Her father sees them off with a shotgun broken across his forearm. He knows the law.

Molly has a knife. With the lowing of a cow in the background, she plunges the point into the pulp of her left index finger. It hurts more than she anticipated, and she drops the knife. The blood wells up, tips over the edge of her nail, and falls to the floor.

Blot, burn, bleach.

No.

Molly waits. At first the carpet buckles inward, as if a drain had formed that sucks in solid objects. Molly's heart hammers. She has never deliberately caused herself to bleed before.

Molly watches as cracks form in the floorboards beneath the carpet. It is a small, slow vortex that sucks in anything around it. This is how the pits form, although she has never seen it. She wonders why and at the same time does not wonder why she has never done this before. She has been asking a lot of questions lately. Who is she? Why does this . . . happen to her? Are other children really like what she sees on television? Is she the only one of her kind? What is life like beyond the fence? Why does hair grow in her armpits?

It is night, and a glistening mass has formed in the pit. A transparent membrane of sorts covers it, and deep within something flexes and relaxes. It is the size of a football.

"Molly! Supper!" calls her mother.

"I'm not hungry," she says.

"You never eat anymore," her mother says in a lower register.

She sucks her finger, keeps her vigil, wondering if a molly can form from the blood she swallows. That would kill her—a molly bursting through her belly. Molly falls asleep.

When she wakes the molly is fully formed and standing by the bedside, watching her sleep. It is only just dawn, and the room is brighter. The floor is ruined, excavated almost through to the level below.

"Molly," says Molly, "get dressed."

~

To get on a bus you need money; Molly does not know exactly how much, but she has been stealing from her parents for six months now. She has planned this. When she steps over the fence it feels frightening but exhilarating. She is the Man in the Iron Mask escaping from her prison of Laws. She hikes for a mile, staying off the road but following it. She goes eastward. She comes to a small shelter that seems to be a bus stop. She feels exposed here. Her father or the mailman might drive past, although she is wearing a hood and has packed her long black hair into a bun.

A bus arrives. She takes out a denomination and surrenders it to the driver, who swears under his breath before rooting out change. Molly sits at the back. There is only one other person on the bus, a woman, who glances at Molly once before ignoring her for the rest of the ride.

The first sign of the town itself is the spire of some church that appears over the trees. It plays peekaboo as the bus negotiates a winding road. They cross a stone bridge and all of a sudden they are in the town.

"Last stop," says the bus driver.

At first Molly does not move. It is the middle of the day, almost exactly noon. People are everywhere, and nothing has prepared Molly for the number, the variety, the vitality, of others. The varied skin shades, the smell of their bodies as they waft past, the sounds of their voices, the swish of their wheelchairs, the smoke of their automobiles.

Molly follows behind a group of elderly women, listening to their voices. It's not like on TV. People speak without purpose, interrupt one another, and trail off. Neither of her parents is a big talker, so Molly drinks these spoken words in. There are tall people, short people, thin, fat, old, young, bland, colorful. There are cut flowers, though not as good as her mother's. She walks past a shop window and sees herself. There is a smile on her face. A statue comes to life, and she squeals when she realizes it is a man coated, clothes and all, in metallic paint. A woman with flowers in her hair makes elongated bubbles in the breeze. Molly stops to talk to a homeless man who spends fifteen minutes showing her exactly how to insulate a coat using found materials, mostly crumpled-up newspapers. She wanders into a building that turns out to be a library. Under "Local Interest" she finds a chapbook that explains the founding of the town. The history turns out to be the same as that of most other places she has studied: war, peace, resources, and settlement. A boy around her age walks past, stares, smiles, then keeps walking. Molly's throat tightens.

She likes the hush of the library, so she stays and reads for a while. She tries to get a library card, but she has no ID. Molly leaves when the librarian asks her what school she attends, not wanting the attention.

The sky has turned slightly grey and there are darker

clouds gathering. Molly buys street food from a van and eats while she explores art shops and psychics and animal cruelty campaigners. She has her portrait done in charcoal by an art student.

Then she turns around, clutching the cylinder of cartridge paper, and there stands her father.

"Hello, Molly. Get in the truck."

Molly doesn't say anything, silenced by the disappointment on his face. It has a purity that frightens her.

"Seat belt," he says. He fusses with the keys.

She pulls the belt into the catch, and when it clicks into place she senses movement. Too late she sees her father stab her with a needle and depress the plunger at the same time. She drives the heel of her palm into the angle of his jaw and feels it give—dislocated. She follows through with a slap to the front of his neck, but her hand seems like it is made of felt. She falls asleep.

She wakes up unable to move. Before she opens her eyes she can tell from the smell that she is in the barn on Southbourne Farm. She can smell blood too. On the ground in front of her, two dead mollys.

Molly's arms are bound behind her with plastic ties. She is seated with her back against the wall. One of the lights is on, and her father stands there with a rifle in his hand and a bandage looping over the crown of his head, holding his jaw in place.

"I think," says her father, "that you might be the real Molly. You don't seem to have gone bad."

"I'm sorry for hitting you, Daddy."

"The police are coming to check on you. Two mollys made it to town. I had to find them and . . . The police want to make sure everything is okay, that we aren't molesting you. Child Protection and all that. Your mother and I were very concerned—we put a missing person call out."

"Untie me. I'll explain to the police that I just ran away."

"Molly, why did you run? We could have been hurt. We could have hurt you, or worse, killed you."

"I wanted to see the town."

"I told you it's dangerous to—"

"It is also glorious! I love what I saw today, what I ate, the people I talked to. Living on this farm isn't living at all if I can't—"

"Two mollys were closing in on you, you wee shite. I got them off your back; you didn't even know they were following you while you were basking in your glorious afternoon."

Molly is dutifully polite to the police. They leave without incident.

~

A fortnight later she kills for the first time. This begins a period of difficult behavior. Molly allows the mollys to live, only to kill them for sport. She sometimes asks them questions before killing them.

"Where do you come from?"

"Why do you hate me?"

"*Do* you hate me?"

"Why?"

"What will you do if I set you free?"

"What do you remember before today?"

"Do you love me?"

"*Do you love me?*"

She perplexes her parents as she disposes of a vast number of mollys. In these teenage years she kills three mollys a week, sometimes as many as one a day. She discards the rules. She allows her monthlies to become a problem for her parents. She is angry and doesn't know why. She begins to cut herself, at first for the purpose of generating mollys, but later because cutting her thighs gives her relief from the nameless pain inside her.

"Why do you find it so easy to kill me?" she asks her father. "You must hate me."

"They are not you, darling." But this is futile, she does not listen.

Her parents fear her too—she sees this in their hesitancy and the gingerly way their speech probes at her psyche. Her body develops under the influence of their training as well as pubertal hormones. Yes, her breasts appear and her hips widen, but she becomes wiry and rangy. She takes regular expeditions into town. She is sort of seeing a boy by the time she is fifteen.

The emotional turbulence, the cutting, and the sport killing die down almost overnight when she turns seventeen. She kills only when there are mollys made by mistake. She feels calm again, or resigned. She helps around the farm and talks to her parents again, actual conversations of more than three words.

~

This is not a night that Molly can sleep through. She has her curtains pulled open, and the moon, full as it is, effortlessly lights up her room in a pale grey-blue.

She sits up in her bed, and her heart is not just going fast, it seems to be accelerating, which is impossible. Molly knows the parameters of the heart from her lessons. Under the covers she is fully dressed. Her shoes wait in formation for her feet to quicken them. The light changes, and Molly looks up. Clouds mute the lunar illumination.

When the first pebble hits her window she is out of bed and into her shoes. Outside, William stands poised to throw another pebble. Molly imagines she can see his smile from where she is. She closes the curtains and opens the bedroom door. Foresight is oiling the dead bolt, latch bolt, and hinges with WD-40 earlier in the day. She runs on tiptoes down the corridor, slides down the banister, and slips out the back door of the house. The moon lights her way. She beckons to William and he crushes against her for a few seconds, before they run down the slope at the back of the property to the banks of the stream.

Kissing first. Lots of kissing. Molly spends a lot of time with her eyes on the imposing silhouette of the farmhouse, waiting for a light to pop on and her father to yell her name, but then she gets properly into the moment. He is hesitant, but she explores everything that catches her fancy. She inhales his breath.

"Molly—" Voice heavy with lust.

"Tonight, William, now. *A thousand honey secrets shalt thou know.*"

It is cold, but they learn the secrets of love and pain, pleasure and blood. It both is and is not everything Molly expects. The books she studied in preparation don't prove useful. The romance books are too metaphorical, the sex books too mechanical.

"You're quiet," says William. The gurgle of water over stones and the high-pitched complaint of a fox surround them.

"Just thinking."

"Are you . . . sorry?"

"No."

"Then what are you thinking?"

"I'm thinking I want to do it again. But not now."

"You realize you talk funny, right?" says William.

"I haven't been around many people and I grew up in a linguistically static environment. I understand what you mean. I watch TV to keep my idioms and colloquialisms up-to-date, but it obviously hasn't worked."

"You've been on the farm all your life?"

"Yes."

"That's insane. Listen to this."

He places the left earbud of his headphones in her ear. The music is loud, grinding metal. She struggles to find the harmony at first, and uses the percussion as a key. Through all that power, a pattern emerges, and she likes it.

"Do you have more?" she asks.

William laughs. "You want more of everything."

"We're only alive for a short time. We should live while we're alive."

William starts to talk about the Ravenala palm he is trying to grow, but Molly stops listening. She is already thinking of disposal.

If you bleed, blot, burn, and bleach.

"Time to go, William."

"When will I see you?"

"I'll come to the library. Day after tomorrow."

Molly waits while his shadow flits and disappears, then she soaks the linen she brought in bleach. It takes half an hour for her to be satisfied, then she goes back to bed with a throbbing soreness between her legs. She takes the time to write William a free verse poem before dozing off.

When she wakes there is a molly standing over her. It drips with water from the stream and it is muddy up to its ankles. Its hair is plastered to its skull.

Molly sighs. *"What follows more she murders with a kiss."*

She gets out of bed.

~

Molly knocks at her mother's door and peeps. Her mother is on the bed, seated.

"Dad said you wanted to see me?"

"Yes. Come. Sit."

"What do you need?"

"Dad said he walked in on you the other day."

"Oh . . ."

"He said you had a molly."

"I didn't do anything wrong."

"He said you were touching its genitals."

"I was only looking. I was curious."

"I understand, *dorogoy*. You haven't done anything wrong."

"Then why are we having this conversation?"

"Baby, don't play with the mollys. They are dangerous."

"I know. Can I go now?"

~

Every week Molly and her mother take a one-day hike with a fully loaded backpack, regardless of the season. They take no food, and only a liter of water each, in canteens. The packs are weighted with rocks.

"When I was young, I was made to do this without a backpack or water." She ruffles Molly's hair before binding it in a silk scarf. "Entitled bitch."

"Why were you made to?"

"Training."

They begin their walk north. As usual, the first thing they do is hack branches off a tree for use as all-purpose sticks. They each have a hunting knife.

"Tell me about the training," says Molly. She times her breathing with her stride. Usually her mother likes to be silent on the hikes, as if worried about alerting an enemy or stalker.

"They dropped us ten miles from a base camp with a compass and a hunting knife. My trainer said that in his day they weren't even given a compass or knife. The first order of the day was to find flint or iron pyrite, or some material to make a stone knife."

She talks of random things. How to seal a lean-to with mud, leaves, and dirt. How to make fire. How to leave food stores for your journey back. Edible insects. Trapping. How to purify water using the clothes off your back.

"In a tropical environment, if you are under a harsh sun, you can use banana leaves as sunglasses by puncturing them and looking through them. Tree bark also works for this. Same technique works for snow blindness."

Molly takes note of all of this, memorizing it without giving outer indication. When they stop for lunch Molly kills and skins the rabbit they trap. Perhaps because of the information her mother shared, Molly tries to prove herself. She cuts herself by mistake. This is the first cut she has ever had on a hike, and when her mother tries to assist Molly shrugs her off. She feels angry at her mother's lean muscles.

"Baby, *dorogoy,* do not rush these things. You cannot

force enlightenment. The flower blooms when it is ready, not when you want it to, and that is why you bleed."

They dispose of the blood together, mother and daughter. This far away from Southbourne Farm a molly would be lost, although secretly Molly wishes to find out if it can find its way home.

⁓

Ugh. Shaving.

Molly decides she will not be shaving her legs, armpits, or anywhere else blighted by puberty.

Her mother laughs at this notion, but does not disagree with her.

⁓

Molly sneezes. She feels misery to her core and she does not care. She hates having a cold. She feels so congested that she cannot be bothered with the rules. Her father stands vigil over her because of her tendency toward nosebleeds.

"Most people in the village think your mother is a mail-order bride, because of her accent. She isn't. Mykhaila was born here, in this country, but moved abroad when she was very young."

When her father talks of Mother is the only time Molly hears his voice soften. He seems made of and from the farm itself: hard, craggy, but nourishing. Always working.

A farm works even while it sleeps, dorogoy. The plants are pushing crops out of the ground, the hens are making eggs, the cows are lactating for imaginary offspring, the worms and insects and bacteria are churning the soil.

What Molly hates most about having a cold is that she cannot read. Her brain feels swollen and sluggish. Her eyes water and her nose drips more when she tries to read.

"Read to me, Daddy."

"What do you want to hear?"

"The Comedy of Errors."

As he reads, Molly gets drowsy and falls asleep.

∼

Molly has her back to the bathroom door, her feet anchoring it shut. Her toes are splayed and her heels dug into the cold tiles. Outside, the mollys hit the door and the force is transmitted to her shoulders. Her feet move a fraction of an inch each time. A pool of blood spreads from the other side of the door and is advancing toward her feet. She is aware that when the puddle reaches her heels it will lubricate them, and she will no longer be able to brace the door.

She sighs.

She shivers with a fever and all her muscles ache. Her nose is only slightly congested, but her joints are pure agony. She cannot concentrate well, and has a headache—throbbing and true. She would surrender to death if only the mollys would stop banging on the fucking door. She just wants to catch her breath. She coughs, but her throat seems to tangle and she gags. Dry heave. No vomit. All fluids gone after seven days of her flu. It has made her careless, but she does not care. She wants to lie down and die. She looks around the bathroom for the first time, searching for a weapon. She could rip off the shower curtain and use the rod as a bo staff, but she doesn't know if she can do it between leaving the door and them charging in. The toilet's cistern cover is heavy ceramic, old-fashioned and thus heavy, but slow. Slow as the advance of blood from the other side of the door.

There is a cabinet. It might have noxious cleaning products for a makeshift pepper spray. Or pepper splash. Molly feels sixty percent sure that there is bleach in there. Her parents' bathroom. Unfamiliar. Both of them out on a date—a date, no less! Who'd have thought? They took one look at her face and wished to cancel, but Molly forbade them. Then she vomited on her own bed and relocated to theirs, promptly falling asleep.

Then, then, then.

Surrounded by mollys, fuck knows where from, fight, fight, fight, aim for the bathroom en suite.

Bang, bang, bang!

"All right!" she says. "All right."

Molly takes a breath, coughs, and leaps away from the door, slips, and falls face first. She sees stars and can feel blood trickling down her nostrils. She can hear them scrambling behind her and feels a hand circle her ankle. She is a foot from the cabinet. She looks around—three naked mollys, climbing over one another to get to her. Blood drenched, one has shat herself for some reason, eyes widened, mouths open in a kind of soundless scream. With her other leg, she kicks the one who has hold of her, then she lunges forward, pulling herself to the cabinet. She flings the door open just as she feels a jolt of white heat in her back—the bitch bit her! The inside of the cabinet is dark, but Molly reaches and her hand wraps around her salvation.

She flips over and pistol-whips the closest molly—impact on the temple—then she checks the safety and shoots the molly's face off. In the close quarters it almost punctures her eardrums. She shoots the second in the chest and the third in the thigh. *Thigh wounds can be mortal because of the femoral artery.* Two more head shots and Molly allows herself to fall to the floor. She feels the blood trickle down her back from the bite.

Don't bleed.

If you bleed, blot, burn, and bleach.

If you find a hole, find your parents.

Molly returns to the cabinet for bleach.

There are twelve dead mollys in different death poses all around the bedroom. Plus the three in the bathroom, that makes fifteen. Molly splashes bleach over all of them and wishes them a happy hereafter, a perverse libation.

When her parents arrive she is lying on a pile of corpses she'd been trying to clean. The flu and her exertion have left her weak beyond her own imaginings. She can barely move her eyeballs to track her horrified parents. Her mother, resolute, gives her a thick, black liquid she calls ASD, which stands for "antiseptic *dorogova*." Molly hates it, and senses that it is a source of tension between her parents, because her father has this disapproving look on his face all the while her mother prepares it.

Later, they give her ice cream, chocolate first, then strawberry, because that is all she can keep down. She sleeps between them, like when she was much younger, and wakes up in her own bed, clean and dry, with no pain in her muscles or joints.

∽

Molly hides behind a tree and watches her father. She watches the dogs play around him as he moves from task to task. She sees him crouch, clutch the soil in both hands, and spend minutes staring at it in the morning sun, then raise the clump to his nose as if smelling it. What is he doing? Every day, his actions seem like he is experiencing life anew. When he comes in for lunch it is the same. He eats the stroganoff like he has never tasted it before, and he stares at Molly's mother like he has never seen her before, like he loves her with the love in poems.

"You aren't eating," says her mother.

Ma isn't any better than her father, and seems to find poetry in bookkeeping. She starts the day with Molly, teaching her how to make her punch more effective. Keeps talking about the second knuckle, about keeping her wrist and elbow aligned, even when punching in a curve. "One of my Chinese instructors told me every punch is part of a circle," she says.

Molly is practicing short jabs in the air. "What about straight punches?"

"*Dorogoy,* a straight line is the curve from a circle of infinite radius."

Molly does not fully understand, but keeps her jabs short and snappy, like her mother instructs.

After an hour and a half of practice she assigns Molly schoolwork and retreats to her study to do farm accounts. Molly, by this time, finds the work so easy that she finishes in half the time, then creeps up on her mother, staring at her from corners and door cracks, or listening to her. She is just like her father. Too much joy, too much pleasure from the banal.

Molly starts an elaborate diary documenting her parents' every action and word. At first she does not know why, but after some weeks she becomes convinced they are not her parents. They look exactly like them, down to their scars, and they wear the same clothing, but the more Molly observes them, the more she believes that they are duplicates, like the mollys. She takes her time looking for her real parents. She systematically digs up the fallow side of the farm using a grid system, looking for graves. On one such excursion she finds the bones of three children—mollys, no doubt—and she is spooked. She continues her search. She cannot find her parents, and because she is worried, she arms herself. She feels she can either subdue or at least delay her father, but her mother is too skilled. Molly has never been able to best her in sparring, and she knows her mother usually holds back.

"It's like chess. You improve more when your opponent is slightly better than you. Only slightly."

Molly carries a small steak knife on her person, to even the odds. Her mother keeps the hunting knives locked up until the hike days, so that isn't an option.

At night, Molly feels she can hear them talking about her. One winter morning she is convinced that her father plans to stab her with a butter knife. It's in the way he holds it while talking Molly through her history lessons. She is determined that he will not get her first. She pulls her knife from the waistband of her shorts and stabs her father in the forearm. The butter knife clatters to the floor. Her father looks more shocked than hurt. Molly remembers her training. *When you stab someone, pull the knife free, otherwise you are unarmed, plus you've given your enemy a weapon.*

Her mother is very still. "Is she one of the . . . ?"

"I don't know. I thought she looked tense." Her father covers the wound with a dishcloth. A sheen of sweat appears on his forehead, but he does not cry out.

"Where are my parents?" screams Molly.

"What?" asks her father.

Molly lunges for him. She bounces off a force field. She is confused until she realizes her mother is between them, and has kicked her in the chest. Her mother's copy. She subdues Molly and ties her up using strips of the tablecloth.

Her father leaves the room and returns with Molly's

diary. "Listen to this: *The fetch, double, wraith, or doppelgänger are related concepts of human duplication in English, Irish, or German folklore. Seeing one usually means the death of the original. What if I am the wraith, the fetch, or the doppelgänger? I kill all the mollys I see.*" He reads out the surveillance logs.

"Oh, sweetheart," says her mother.

～

Weeks of drugs. Medication. No hospitalization, but a doctor is brought to the farm.

"Capgras Syndrome," says the doctor. "The unshakable belief that people around you have been replaced by doubles."

Molly believes him, after the medication. She is better in six weeks, and begins to trust her parents again.

Her mother says she is impressed with the level of detail Molly included in the logs.

～

"You should write a book about this," says her father.

Molly listens to her parents talking to each other, kidding, giggling. She is lying on the roof on a hot, balmy summer night. She cannot sleep for the sweat and humidity, and neither can her parents. They have thrown open the windows and are content. Theirs is the talk of lovers, full of shorthand, snorted laughter, and sentences completed by the other. Some of it Molly cannot understand, but she is happy just hearing them so. She is satisfied that everything is right and good.

She is mostly surrounded by darkness. Her back is cooled by the roofing slats and the sky is made of ink, with an untamed spray of glitter, the Milky Way. At times a blinking light will crawl across, a high-altitude airplane, a satellite, a UFO, or the heart of Molly's true love. The wind rustles her hair, blows it into her face. She brushes it away and tucks it under her head.

Her parents are talking about how they met. The story comes in stops and starts, and Molly has to piece it together in her head.

Her father is already a farmer. The land is passed to him from his own father, and he has grown up learning how to work the land. After a brief flirtation with the humanities, Connor is resigned to his role. One day a car pulls up when none is expected. It is her mother. She stands in the driveway, shouting, "Hello?" Either one or both of the dogs they have at the time run up, but instead of barking they lick her hands. Her father appears, covered in mud. He has been tinkering with a tractor—replaced before Molly is born. Mykhaila starts to speak in what she thinks is English, but her father cannot understand because of her thick accent. He thinks she is complaining about something. She is actually saying she has noticed that a lot of the fresh produce in the town is from Southbourne Farm and she would like to come directly to the source. He asks if she would like a cup of tea, and she nods.

He washes himself and meets her in the house. He notices the absence of a wedding ring. Such things mattered back then. He says she uses eyeliner in a manner different from that of the local girls. It makes her eyes stand out, and he stares. He does not speak much, and when he does it is direct and without hesitation. He establishes what she wants over the course of four cups of tea. She lives in a rented room in a cottage and when he asks about a partner she demurs. When he says he would like to call on her like in the nineteenth-century novels, she smiles. Their romance begins a month after the meeting.

An owl hoots somewhere, and there is a flurry of movement that makes Molly think it is hunting.

Molly is born in the house, with help from a visiting midwife and doula. By this time her mother lives on Southbourne, and her parents are so much in love. They do not speak of the time after the birth, and they both seem to go quiet, enveloped by one of those silences that develop between them, a telepathic moment from which

Molly is excluded. When their sounds change to something she knows she should not be privy to, she makes her way across the roof and works herself over the edge, onto the pipe that brought her up.

Soon she is asleep in her bed.

$\sim$

"This is a bad idea," says her mother.

"Why? You went to college," says Molly.

"I did not have your condition."

"You did not have my parents, either," says Molly. They touch noses and smile. Love.

"What do you want to study?"

"I don't know. Literature? Genetics?"

Her mother smiles.

"What's funny?"

"I was just remembering myself in college, that's all. How will you protect yourself?"

"The way you have taught me."

$\sim$

Molly's scores on the interviews are good enough to get her into the best three universities in the country. The one she chooses was established a thousand years prior by a religious secret society intent on directing the path of the nation through a small pool of elite families and a smattering of commoners who showed uncommon intellectual spark. The institution prides itself on having produced scores of heads of state and international prizewinners. None of this features in Molly's decision making. She chooses this particular place because the entire town rests on catacombs full of ancient and modern books, a fact she finds magical. On the day her parents drop her off there is a violent clash between the police and student protesters over a demonstration about one of the more prestigious scholarships being named after a known racist and supporter of genocide.

"I don't like this," says her father. "We should turn back."

"We're not turning back. We just drove four hours. Let's just find the hall of residence and unpack," says Molly from the backseat.

"Tear gas and water cannon. It's good to be back," says her mother.

She has a room to herself because of a negotiated position with the administration due to a fabricated medical condition. Molly is amused that her mother knows how to forge documents to prove the presence of hemophilia. By the time she has unpacked, the violence has fizzled out and the sun is barely visible on the horizon. It is colder, and watching her parents' taillights recede makes her realize she is truly happy only when they are around. *"The tumult and the shouting dies; / The Captains and the Kings depart . . ."* She murmurs this without thinking, homesick already.

~

Molly finds her first exposure to formal education underwhelming, and many of her co-students lazy. Perhaps a third of them do the reading before the lectures, while she had read most of the recommended texts prior to the first day. Her questions are the most convoluted, but engage and interest the professors. She enjoys her studies, but not her academic interactions with the students.

There is a student across the hall from Molly called Adele. She has said exactly one sentence to Molly.

"Oh, you're the hemophilia girl." Adele walks away after this.

On the weekend, Molly notices a lot of voices coming from Adele's room. She opens the door and looks out. There is a man in the corridor waiting while Adele hugs a little human. It makes Molly uncomfortable. Just before she can escape back into her room Adele's eyes fly open, and she shrieks, "Molly! Come meet my son, Brian!"

Molly panics and slams her door shut.

She cannot stand children. They remind her of the

mollys, with their innocence and their half-formed personalities, and she expects them to burst into violence any minute. They never do, but they might. Her nightmares are always about children in some way. Every time she finds herself in the presence of a child she has to suppress the urge for a preemptive strike. She has previsualized this so many times, and it frightens her.

She hears the child laugh, among peals of delight from the adults. The child being fetishized is not a surprise given its rarity. With falling fertility rates, any baby is a cause for celebration. And yet Adele calls over Molly, a woman she barely knows, to demonstrate her fecundity. *Show-off.*

Fuck Adele and fuck children for being creepy.

She has the mollys, and they are not rare. She does not fetishize them. They do not grow. Are the mollys her children? Is she capable of having children the normal way? Can she get pregnant? She has always been careful, but now she wonders if each molly that she kills depletes her ovaries. Will she even want children?

Hemophilia girl can't breed because she has a blood disease.

∽

"Can I see your notes for Crewe?"

Molly looks up. There's a guy hovering over her with raised eyebrows. He's got a boring sweater on, but the chill has brought color to his cheeks. He is not unpleasant to look at, and Molly likes his voice.

"You weren't in Crewe," she says. She knows every face in her lectures. Her mother has taught her to quickly scan crowds and recognize the unfamiliar.

"That's why I need the notes."

"You have never been in Professor Crewe's lectures."

"Again, that's why I always need notes."

"Can you get them back to me in four hours?"

"Why four hours?"

"My review pattern. I reread the notes immediately after a lecture, six hours later, and twenty-four hours after that. Retention reinforcement."

"Interesting technique. I'll need to try it."

"Not if you don't attend lectures."

She lets him take her notebook from the table. While he flips through the leaves she finishes her coffee.

"Lavinia as property? I thought Crewe forbade feminist readings of *Titus Andronicus*."

"He does. This isn't a feminist reading. She was property, first claimed by Bassianus like a sack of flour, *suum cuique*. Before that she existed for the benefit of Titus, for him to bestow upon whichever ruler would benefit him the most."

"Crewe thinks it's of its time."

"And we are of ours. We should read it as such. What's your name?"

"Leon."

"Will you bring my notes back on time, Leon?"

"Give me your address."

~

He comes on time and drops off the book. He has not torn the pages or left coffee rings on it. After he leaves, Adele comes by.

"Be careful of that guy. He's not enrolled here," she says. The incident of the baby lies unmentioned between them like a family secret.

"Where does he study?"

"He doesn't. He's a townie. He targets freshmen every year. Watch out."

~

Molly thinks of Lavinia, husband killed, claimed as spoils, raped by two Goths, hands cut off, tongue cut out so she cannot speak, and finally killed by her own father. Molly does not understand how honor works for men, but she has wanted to murder Titus Andronicus since she first read the play when she was twelve. Not metaphorically: she remembers wishing he were a real, live human so she could kill him. Professor Crewe is daft; she can barely concentrate in his class.

Leon has left his number in her notes.

⁓

Molly surprises Leon at his home address. At first he does not let her in, but she pushes past. There is a girl in his front room.

"Get out," Molly says.

"Hey," says Leon.

"You want to fuck freshers? We can fuck as much as you want, as often as you want. Get rid of her, she's not going to sleep with you."

Later, while they are moving against each other, she fantasizes about cutting off his hands and tongue.

After some weeks, Leon says, "I love you, Molly."

"No, you don't, you silly sausage. You think you're in love because I'm emotionally unavailable. You'll get over it."

⁓

Surprisingly, her father writes to her first. Up until the moment she rips open the envelope postmarked from her hometown, she thinks it is from her mother.

Dear Molly,

It is unusual not hearing you root about in the house. I did not know how comforting that sound was until your mother and I returned home. We still did the same things, I the heavy lifting and your mother the paperwork, but it wasn't the same. Last night we had our first argument in years. It was about nothing, but I suspect it is residue from the emotional backwash of dropping you off. Empty nest, maybe. We don't know what to do with your room. Clean it? Tidy it? Both? Neither? Your mother's ambivalence shows in everything.

I miss you so much. I have seen you every day for so long.

I shall have to get a hobby to take my mind off all of this. Any suggestions?

With love
Your father

She writes back, describing her room, talking about Adele and her accursed spawn, skipping Leon, discussing her lectures and the eccentricities of her lecturers. Her letter runs to seven pages. She rereads his letter every night, which surprises her. She is not usually given to sentimentality.

~

James Down is a professor of physiology and anatomy. He knows everything in his field. Molly has never seen him falter when a student asks a question. She checks the answer each time, and Down is always right. He is the international authority on renal blood flow patterns. His paper on variations in arterial blood flow to the head of the femur is seminal. He is animated when talking about the lateral circumflex femoral artery. Molly notes that his eyes are wider at these times.

Dorogoy, *always look at the eyes. This is the best way to anticipate attacks.*

When she queues up behind other students to ask a question whose answer she knows, she realizes she wants him.

With Leon, she imagines fucking James Down, and she comes so violently that she flexes her thighs too powerfully. Leon is hurt, although he assures her that nothing is broken. She can tell from his strutting afterward that he feels responsible for her pleasure. She does not disabuse him of this notion.

She makes her own way back to her dorm, slips into the darkness of her suite. She is locking the door when a shove to the back of her head smacks her face into the wood panel. She sees stars, feels her nose broken, kicks behind her, misses, and turns.

The molly is just beyond kicking distance. It has tied its hair into a fucking bun. How long has it been—

A fist slams into Molly's chin. She raises her forearms just in time to weather the further punches. *This molly is fast.*

Molly's brain is so rattled, she cannot think of a defense or fighting strategy. The molly kicks her in the right knee, then pulls her hair. Molly is ready for the punch coming from the other side, but it is a feint. The molly leaves the hair and sticks a finger into Molly's eye, then, when Molly is blind, smashes her in the ribs with what might be an elbow strike.

Need to get out of this. Cornered. Open this fight up. Ignore pain. Ignore blindness. Do something unexpected.

She drop-kicks the molly. Her feet connect. Hope. She hears the clatter across the room. She opens her watery eyes and sees the molly rise and charge again. Molly sidesteps and slams the molly into the door. She kicks it between the legs from behind. It has its fucking chin tucked in, even when hurting. Molly kicks it in the lower back, then spins, kicking its head. It's not unconscious, but it's slowed and incapacitated. Molly grabs it by the right arm and twists in the wrong direction until it dislocates. She does the same for the left. She gets a knife from the kitchen and runs into another molly.

～

The mantra doesn't work here. She is bleeding, there is not enough bleach, and she cannot call her parents.

It takes four hours to clean up. Molly has never had to fight this hard. The mollys seem to be more intense, more focused. Does that have to do with being at the university? Does thinking hard make mollys more acute? She found a third one under the bed. Cunning too?

She cleans herself up as much as possible, wraps the bodies in sheets, and waits until dark for disposal.

She knows she is not well. It hurts to breathe, and she feels on the verge of blacking out. She manages to lock her room, stagger to Adele's door, and knock.

"Help me," she says.

～

As she lies in the hospital bed, she knows the mollys will come for her. She has bled too much, and has no control over where the multiple dressings go. Most will be destroyed as biohazardous, but she counts on the incompetence of others. Mollys always grow. They always find a fucking way to surprise her.

All these years. *How have I survived?*

Why have I survived? This cycle will repeat itself.

There are levels of pain that preclude conscious thought. Pain so pure that the world falls away and your primal caveperson self calls out to primordial gods for relief or death.

Slaves in pre-colonial Congo were once used for ritual sacrifices in which all their bones were broken, and they were left to die. *Imagine their pain, yours is not so bad.* Abstracting the pain helps, but not much.

The despair evaporates when she hears the pounding on the door of her room.

She wraps one end of a chair leg in a bedsheet.

∼

Afterward, all Molly can do is crawl to the nurses' station, trailing blood. She smears the counter as she drags herself up and pulls the first phone she finds over the protests of the ward nurse. It has no outside line. Alarms are going off like the mating calls of robotic insects. The second phone has a dial tone, and Molly calls the number tattooed on her arm.

"Name," says the voice on the line.

"Molly Southbourne."

"Location?"

Molly states the hospital and ward. The handset is slick with body fluids.

"Say nothing. We will be there shortly."

Click.

Molly hangs on to the cord till the nurse takes it from her.

"Good Lord, your ... your fingers are broken," the nurse says.

"You ... should see the other girl," says Molly.

~

About a month later, Molly appears at the local police station. She meets a Detective Cooper. She does not have a lawyer with her, but has been assured this visit is a formality. The interview room is close, about ten by ten, with two cameras on the ceiling. There is a twenty-four-inch TV with an inbuilt cassette slot. Two wall-mounted microphones and a recording device that flashes green while a tape spools inside. There is a three-digit counter that rolls and clicks every second. Cooper is on the other side of the desk, closest to the door.

"Thank you for coming, Miss Southbourne. Am I correct in stating for the record that you are aware of your rights and waive the right to an attorney?"

"That is correct."

"Thank you." He spews some more legalese, but Molly tunes it out. He mentions a date.

"What can you tell me about the events of that date?"

"No comment."

"You were brought in injured, after a vicious assault. Who attacked you?"

"No comment."

"You were further attacked in the hospital. Who attacked you?"

"No comment."

"How many attackers were there?"

"No comment."

"Why was your blood found in copious amounts in your room, the corridor, and three floors down the nearest stairwell?"

"No comment."

"Whose brain tissue was on the chair leg found just outside your room?"

"No comment."

"Surgeons extracted a tooth from your right knuckle. Whose was it?"

"No comment."

"We found an arm ripped or torn or otherwise detached from its owner. The fingerprints are identical to yours. Do you have a twin?"

"No comment."

This goes on for forty minutes, and Molly has frequent flashbacks to the episode, but says nothing. Cooper switches the tape off.

"Miss Southbourne? I've already been told by my superiors that this case is going nowhere and that the evidence is getting lost. You know this, and I know this. Closed file. I just . . . could you tell me what happened here?"

He has an open face. Cut himself shaving, wedding ring, slight waist thickening, looks honest, has not dropped his gaze to her breasts. Yet.

"DC Cooper? No comment. Can I go?"

"You are free to go, ma'am."

~

Molly is back to classes five weeks before Leon finds her. She is cutting into an osteosarcoma when he makes his way into the lab.

"Molly, what the fuck?" His fists are clenched and he's breathing like he ran a marathon.

"You're not allowed in here. This room is for students of anatomy."

"One day you can explain how it makes sense, you studying literature and anatomy. And what the fuck, Molly?"

"What's wrong?"

"The police. They arrested me for assaulting you. They photographed me, questioned me. They thought I was some kind of serial killer or something."

"Don't be dramatic. I didn't know. I'll get you off the hook."

"I'm already off the hook. You haven't called. You haven't studied my anatomy in months."

Ugh. "All these years of associating with freshmen and you can't think of a better line than that? I've been ill, Leon. I've been beaten up. It was not sexy."

"By who?"

"Whom. And it's none of your business."

"What's wrong with whose business?" Professor Down is now in the lab. It's six thirty in the evening, and he should not be there.

"Professor, I'm just catching up," says Molly. Then, sotto voce to Leon, "Leave now, most tedious neighbor."

Exit Leon.

Molly and Down stare at each other.

"Are you busy right now?" Down asks.

"Well . . ."

"I need to dissect a body. It's research. I'm dissecting a

thousand bodies to demonstrate the frequency of mutations in the celiac plexus."

"How many have you done?"

"Three hundred and thirty-two. I'm starting three hundred and thirty-three tonight. Care to assist?"

Molly thinks of three hundred cadavers. She sees hundreds of dead mollys of all ages, but younger than her. Then, like those reincarnation paintings, she sees mollys extending into the future, all ages, old, older. Cancerous mollys, with osteosarcomata.

"Hello? Are you there?" says Down.

"Yes. I do. Care to assist. I care to assist," says Molly.

~

Dear Molly,

I am happy to hear you are making friends. We have always been worried about your social development, being an only child who was homeschooled. Maybe they can come down to the farm for a meal sometime.

Your mother and I are thinking of taking a cruise. We have never been abroad together because of your hemophilia. Now that you have taken flight, I'm ready to see the world. We've hired some people to look after the farm while we are gone.

We found the soakaway of an old outhouse at the back of the property. I'm going to fill it in one of these days. Your mother says we should build a new outhouse instead, more like an art project. . . .

~

After a while, you don't smell the formaldehyde anymore.

Molly finds Down to be deft with a scalpel and she learns what she can from watching him. He keeps up a monologue detailing the history of anatomy, punctuated with questions about a particular nerve or blood supply. He speaks of early resurrectionists as pioneering men on whose shoulders later anatomists stood.

"And women," says Molly.

"What?"

"Some of the 'men' were women pretending to be men." She lists some.

"You are, of course, prepared to provide citations."

"Of course." Molly smiles.

With time Molly comes to handle the scalpel.

"You are comfortable around the dead."

"I grew up on a farm. My father taught me about bodies."

~

The bus stops five miles from Southbourne Farm. Molly jogs cross-country the rest of the way. A good day for running—cool, bright, with motes in the air and the crisp smell of new blooms. An autumn day that aspires to be summer. Even the flies on the turdstools are beautiful.

When she spots her destination she accelerates to a sprint, and there's a light sweat on her by the time she reaches the fence. She stops, catches her breath, peers through the bushes. Silence. The farm is never silent. Some bird trills, but the farm animals are not crying. The house is undamaged, and the front door looks shut, but Molly spots a light on through a second-floor window. Her father would never allow that during the daytime.

Shit. *Shit.* Mommy. Papa.

Molly feels the panic, but does not go in. The house is on a hill. The tactical advantage will be with whoever is in there. Nothing more foolish than rushing into gunfire when she doesn't have to. She is patient. She sits down behind a yew tree, eats a chocolate bar, and waits for nightfall.

Treat the yew with respect, Molly. It is the oldest tree in the country and fucking poisonous to boot. It's associated with legends of both death and immortality.

She does not think of her parents while waiting. She

knows how difficult it is to empty your mind, unless you think of some other thing actively, so she does. She tries to read the novel she brought for the trip, but cannot concentrate on it. She tries to do sums in her head. She recites soliloquies that she can remember. She wishes she could fall asleep, but she has too much nervous energy.

When darkness comes, Molly is over the fence and darting from cover to cover, the way her mother has taught her. Feet light. Short sprints. Conserve energy. The front door is ajar, but she ignores it and goes for the back. It is locked, but she has her keys. She can hear static from a TV set and the refrigerator running. Some creaking of the house settling. The light is on upstairs and Molly heads for it. Every sense is alert, as if even the hairs of her skin have grown as antennae to sense movement.

She passes the kitchen, then doubles back. The fridge is open. All the food wrappers are torn, empty. No food left. She knows then what has happened. She hears the thumping of someone moving upstairs and she goes to meet the molly. She flicks on the corridor light.

At the landing, the molly stops. It is probably three or four years younger than Molly, which means it is an old one that they missed. Its belly is concave and its ribs are prominent, more so with each breath.

"Where are my parents?" asks Molly. No answer.

It comes for her, but it is starved and weak, and Molly

punches it in the chest, cracking the sternum and several ribs. She shoves it down the stairs and goes up to look for her parents.

And finds them.

~

The fucking outhouse.

Maybe Father was going to fill it in or make it into the art project her mother wanted. Either way, he had started digging. The molly was in the hole, must have been there for years, maybe injured. Either Molly or her parents must have thought it dead after a fight. It was there all this time, steadily eating dirt and bugs and grass and petrified shit. Papa set it free and it killed him first. He must have become less vigilant because Molly was at the university. The mess in her mother's room tells Molly she went harder. But she went all the same.

Both bodies have decomposed. Her father's has been partially eaten, though not by the molly. Foxes, stray dogs, something canine.

She buries them both in a plot in town. Certain arrangements are already in play once she calls the number on her arm, and selling the farm is easy. She has long since made the link between these suited people and the "monsters" she used to see as a child. She thinks they might be extra protection arranged for by her parents. Molly has no room to mourn or feel. There is so much to do. The lawyers drop a truckload of papers on her.

She finds a small house on Hogarth Avenue in the city.

~

The house on Hogarth feels right to her. Two floors and a basement. Quiet street, pleasant neighbors who mind their own business. Garden. She hemophiliac-proofs it herself. She spends weeks just sitting in the front room reading a pile of books she has wanted to read forever. She does not mind that she cannot feel anything—she is not ready to deal with her heart yet. Better the lives of fictional people, and the tortuosity of philosophy books. She has sex with a few strangers, but it does not distract her or calm her churning mind, so she stops.

When she finally does feel something, it is not emotional, but physical. She falls sick.

She feels the illness coming on, warned by a nonspecific prodrome. When the vomiting starts, she is not surprised. Her back and muscles ache. Nothing stays in her belly, so she chews ice cubes compulsively. Her bed has no linen—she has just moved in. In a few days the vomiting is accompanied by diarrhea. She sees visions of her parents in her delirium. Her mother, more often. Molly screams her despair and rage at her mother's specter. "You should have killed *me*. I'm the abnormal one, not them. You'd still be alive."

Molly does not wish to go back to the hospital, so she stays still, waiting to die, floating in and out of consciousness. Then, without warning, it is over. Molly feels hunger pangs. She showers and cleans the house. She eats oats raw and washes them down with water. Slowly, she gets her strength back, but her parents are still dead. She reads her father's letters and her mother's writings over and over. So many pages from her mother, but mostly mundane farm accounting shit. Still, it's comforting to read her handwriting.

What next? What do I do?

Molly wants to die, but she knows her mother would not have wanted it. If Mykhaila Southbourne had one religion, it was survival. From before Molly could talk, all she has been told was how to survive.

She scratches herself, but does not break skin. Stay alive. Why? Everyone Molly cares about is dead. She killed them. But she cannot kill herself because of everything her mother had done to get her here.

She gets a steak knife from the kitchen and stabs herself in the forearm. She barely feels it. She floods the wound and floor with thick bleach. Kill it before it grows. She wonders if there are one or two mollys out there, alive, waiting. She stabs herself again, a different spot, still no pain. She should go along the hiking trail, just to be sure. She thinks of ten-, fifteen-year-old mollys, stuck, searching for her, gunning to kill her. Or falling victim to predators—pedophiles, serial killers, careless drivers, pestilence. This does not fill her with pleasure, surprisingly. It is still her, still her body. If anyone is to kill mollys it will be her. She stabs herself again and it hurts. The blood spilling overwhelms the bleach.

She gets more.

~

Professor Down is at the door. How the fuck does he know where Molly lives? He rings the bell again, so Molly draws back the curtain, puts on a housecoat, and goes downstairs. She sniffs both armpits. Not too pungent.

"Professor?" She opens the door only an inch or so.

"Your doorbell is really silent. I couldn't tell if it rang or not."

"I could. Professor—"

"James."

"James, why are you here? How did you know where I live?"

"You haven't been in class. You haven't helped me in our collaboration on celiac plexus mutations. I got curious, asked my secretary to get your address and number.

Then forwarding address. Then . . . you know."

"I dropped out, James."

"Good, does that mean I can ask you out for coffee? I still need an assistant, and you're one of the better ones."

"What? What are you talking about? I'm sick, so no metaphors, please."

James leans in, talks slowly. "I wish to pay you to assist me. I wish to have coffee with you now to discuss the terms."

"I don't want coffee."

"Well, I do. It's cold out here, but I'm a patient god. I'll wait for you to get dressed."

~

"Frankenstein." James says this while chewing on a biscuit. He has tea, not coffee.

"You got into anatomy and physiology because of a movie?"

"Book. Yes, because of Victor Frankenstein."

"When did you read it?"

"I was twelve. I just liked the idea of someone mastering his subject so well that he could take it a step further than anyone else in the field."

"You want to make life?"

"Frankenstein just reanimated body parts he cobbled

together from corpses. He did not make life."

"Says you. Shelley of the miscarriages and child death disagrees with you. What do you want to do?" says Molly.

"I want to know more than my peers." He sips his tea, starts on the last biscuit. "I'll do the work to be that one. I want to know bodies better than anyone else."

"And what will you do with this knowledge?" Molly stares at his stubble, the curve of his Cupid's bow.

"I don't know. I was thinking of sitting on it like a dragon on a pile of gold. I'd wait for questing medical students and postdocs, ambushing them with obscure questions."

"Have you ever opened a cadaver and been surprised?"

James thinks. "Some years ago, in Enugu, I did an autopsy on a guy who died of bowel obstruction. Cut him open, and there, staring back at me, was a red length of cloth tied around his gut."

"You're lying."

"I'm telling you. Just at the splenic flexure. Turns out he'd had surgery before, but offended this surgeon or something, slept with his wife. So the guy ties up his bowel. Takes out the appendix first, though. Very professional purse-string sutures."

Molly does not know whether to believe him or not.

"How long ago was this?"

"I was a year out of university. Haven't been surprised since."

He walks her back and hesitates the way guys do when they want to kiss you, but don't know if they should or if you're attracted. Molly does not make it easy for him.

"I did notice," he says.

"Notice what?"

"You let me talk. You said nothing about yourself."

"My parents just died," she says.

"I'm sorry to hear that." He seems so earnest, it unnerves her.

"I have to go." She opens the door.

"Work for me," he says. It sounds like *Wait for me*.

"Okay."

Three

Before she buys furniture for the house on Hogarth Avenue, Molly sets off in search of a martial arts school. From her time at the university she knows she will never find a teacher like her mother, but she is a good enough student to know that some instruction is better than no instruction. She scrolls through various dojos and dojangs, as well as boxing clubs. She visits every single one on her list. She settles for a mixed martial arts club, and works mostly on her own, but spars once a week. She takes care not to show her true proficiency and smiles when the men go out of their way to teach her techniques she already knows.

~

Employment with the university is not so bad. Her official designation is lab assistant, but built into her contract is the ability to continue her studies in a modular fashion should she wish. She works with James for four hours per day. This generates one hour of paperwork. After that, she can pretty much do what she likes. She loses interest in the courses, though. Even Shakespeare holds no fascination for her.

She has a vague feeling that working with James will at some point equip her to understand the mollys. She does not know how, but human anatomy and physiology are about the only things she can focus on. She has no strong emotions, hasn't since her parents died. She can function, but she is aware of the absence, like a psychic hunger. She looks around for Leon so she can fuck the emptiness away, but she cannot find him. James became businesslike once she accepted the job, and there have been no more invitations to coffee.

She bumps into Adele, says hello, but receives no response. She wants to say thank you to Adele, for saving her that night. Molly knows she should feel regret, but she doesn't.

Regular work reduces the pain of her parents' deaths to an abstract idea. As she cuts the cadavers on the slabs, she realizes there is no sense to be made out of life.

Three or four A.M. Molly opens her eyes as a molly comes into bed with her. It curls up into the hollow of Molly's neck and sobs. Presently, Molly puts her arms around it. With time the weeping stops. It falls asleep and Molly stays in the same position until daybreak. She strokes its hair a few times. An hour after dawn, the molly's muscle tension changes along with its breathing. It wakes.

Here we go again.

～

No matter how careful she is, a molly always appears. How is it that humans bleed so much? Or maybe Molly herself bleeds more than the average human. The rules are useless, an attenuation at best. Lifeblood escapes all the time, minor hemorrhages, a little a day. Maybe that is how we age. Maybe that is how we die.

～

Molly Southbourne dreams that she has a baby. She returns home to find the babysitter gone and the baby shrunk in the Moses basket. When she picks the baby up it is covered in a birth caul, except the caul is made of polyethylene wrap. Within the wrap the baby writhes weakly. There is mucus inside the caul with the child, who looks alive, but grey and diseased. Molly feels like gagging, but she cannot. She tries to scream, but nothing comes out. Then she wakes and a molly is on top of her, face contorted with endless rage, dripping spit and tears onto Molly, its hands tight around Molly's neck. It is still dark in the room, so it's night. The molly is naked, and must have formed within the hour. Molly's blood sings in her ear, so it must have been strangling her for a while. Molly mentally congratulates the molly for choosing a relatively bloodless method.

Her left hand is free, so she punches the molly in the ribs, then thrusts her left hip up sharply. She pushes off the bed with her left foot, hurling them both over the right side. Molly's head hits the nightstand, but at least the stranglehold loosens. Molly sees stars and the lamp is on its side, throwing crazy shapes on the wall. The molly takes a deep breath, steps back to control the distance, then lunges. Molly reaches under the mattress and unsheathes the dagger she has hidden there. When the molly engages Molly swipes for the side of its neck. She is wide of the mark, still seeing stars from lack of oxygen.

The molly blocks her knife hand, cutting Molly's palm and sending the blade away. It punches Molly in the belly, then face. Molly blacks out briefly, but when she opens her eyes the molly is on top of her again. Why is it crying? No air. Might not be a bad time to die. She is about to stop fighting when she starts to see double. No. Not double. A new molly smashes a heavy object (the lamp?) into the one strangling Molly. It strangles the older molly with a gearlock, then snaps its neck. It stands, stares at the body.

Molly picks up the knife and stabs the new molly in the neck. It is not surprised. They are never surprised.

She sits on the carpet, takes ragged breaths. It is 0338 hours. Mollys fighting mollys. Who would have thought?

She splashes thick bleach on the bloodstains, and while she cleans, she wonders if she was born with a caul.

Later, she fires up the autoclave and the furnace.

～

Molly has been at her desk only two hours when Natalie from reception calls to say her sister is at reception.

Natalie babbles: "I don't know, I think she's your sister. She looks exactly like you. Is she your sister?"

"Yes," says Molly.

"Does she have special needs?" Natalie's voice goes up an octave, though the volume drops, like she is inviting a confidence.

"Yes," says Molly.

"What shall I do? She's just standing there. It's weird."

"Keep her there," says Molly. "I'll be down in five minutes."

Molly closes the document she is in the middle of transcribing and locks her screen. She rips off a yellow sticky note and leaves something suitable for James. She expects to be back in a few hours. She gives her desk a once-over. The empty coffee cup is not clean, but she has no time to wash it.

In four minutes she emerges from the lift and sees the reception desk. The molly is there, standing roughly in the position soldiers would call at ease, unmoving. Its clothes do not match, and neither do its shoes, but at least it put some on. If it had walked barefoot Molly does not know how she would have coped with bleeding feet, or explained its nakedness. The molly sees Molly and its eyes widen with recognition.

It smiles, Molly does not. She used to smile at the quiet ones, but she can no longer be bothered. She wants this over and done with.

"Thank you, Natalie," says Molly. She clutches the molly by the forearm and pulls it. It follows Molly into the car and automatically does up its seat belt. It does not talk during the drive home. Some of the mollys can be talkative in their confusion, but they always quiet down before they turn. Molly stays under the speed limit, but only just.

She parks the car and gets the molly out. The time is 1147 hours. She leads it into the house and it follows passively. Molly looks around for the hole, but sees nothing. She will return outside later for a more thorough search. For now she closes the front door after a quick glance. Nobody is watching.

"Are you hungry?" asks Molly.

"I could kill for some tea," it says. It is something Molly says often.

Molly puts the kettle on, then leads the molly to a chair.

"Cream? Sugar?" Molly asks, but she knows the answer. Yes to both.

She stares briefly at the whorls of hair at the back of the molly's head, then she reaches into a drawer and puts on workman's gloves. They are yellow, stained, and oversize.

"Isn't this nice," says the molly.

"Yes," says Molly. "It is."

Then Molly flips the garrote wire over the molly's head and pulls. She is unimpressed by its struggles, and falls back while keeping the wire taut. Noises come from the molly. It kicks and thrashes. Molly remains still and waits. Even after the molly stops gurgling and jerking, Molly waits for another ten minutes.

She shoves the body off her, pulls the wire free where it has dug into the neck, and waits for any movement. She feels for a pulse, opens the eye, and pokes it. No reaction.

She opens a cabinet and selects a jug of industrial bleach and lime. She drops the garrote into a basin and splashes bleach enough to immerse it. There is a little blood around the neck of the molly, but all in all, it is a neat job. She cleans the neck with bleach. She can find no blood on the floor. Just to be sure, she flips the lights on in the kitchen. Molly pulls off the tablecloth and drops it over the face of the molly. She cleans her hands carefully, checks her hands for cuts and blood smears. Finding none, she nods and leaves the house. She walks around the house and finds the hole at the back. She makes a note to buy seventy kilos of soil on her way home.

She will deal with the body when she comes back from work.

~

Molly works without a break for three hours to make up for the time away from her desk. She is about to start on a fresh report when James hovers. She takes the earbuds out and looks up at him.

"You're . . . er, you're working?" asks James.

"Yes, that's what I'm paid to do," says Molly.

"Right. Right. I . . . er . . . heard your sister came in. I didn't know you were a twin."

"She's very quiet, but she misses me a lot. She doesn't understand the city. We're from the country," says Molly.

"Right. Right."

Molly does not know how to flirt, although she wishes

she did. She has always known this time would come with James, but she had wanted to get close to him more naturally. She knows he wants to ask her out, but he is a professor and a nerd. Generally shy outside of his chosen field. She will have to initiate.

"James," she says.

"Yes?"

"Would you like to have a drink after work?"

"I would like that very much."

~

Molly returns home.

She fills the hole with soil from the gardening center. She knows the molly grew from where she threw the remnants from her monthlies. Which is odd, because she takes precautions against that kind of thing. Inside, she lays polyethylene sheets on the floor of her kitchen, then she carefully carves the corpse, the way her father taught her, the way James taught her. The head in one piece. She cuts off the arm at the shoulder joint, starting from the armpit and working her way around. Each arm she divides at the elbow and wrist joint. She takes off each leg at the hip joint, then separates the knee joint tendons. The ankle is fiddly, and even though she knows how to do it, she is in a hurry and does not bother.

She makes a Y incision on the trunk and empties the viscera into a bucket.

She treats all the parts with bleach, then lime. She mixes the blood with a chlorine powder that she sourced from a factory outlet.

She takes the parts to her furnace and lights it.

Molly strips off all her clothes and gloves. She puts them in her personal autoclave and starts the sterilization process.

She stops the plug in the bathtub and washes herself with a dilute bleach solution, then she steps out. She treats the collected water, then, satisfied, she drains it.

She showers again, gets dressed, and leaves for her date with James.

～

James is already in the restaurant. Their arrangement morphed from a drink to a meal as the workday progressed because neither James nor Molly likes bars. He has already finished two glasses of wine by the time Molly arrives. He offers a glass, but she declines. He is still wearing his jacket from work, but the shirt is different. He has also polished his shoes. This is important to him. Molly knows because she has seen him prepare for conferences in the same way. Most of the time he wears the first thing that he sees when he opens his eyes. Brilliant mind, but not great at grooming.

He is talking at her.

"What?" says Molly.

"I said, you look really good tonight."

"Thank you, James."

"I like your cheekbones. Slavic ancestry?"

"I don't know. My mother spoke some Russian and Ukrainian, but I don't know."

"Did you know the word *slave* comes from Slavs because they used to be taken into slavery a lot?"

"Yes, I did. James, can I be honest with you? I don't do small talk well, and I want to tell you something."

"All right."

"Let's get the pressure out of the way first. I will sleep with you. Not because I want something from you, though I do. I'll sleep with you because I like you. I like your unfashionable clothes and your eyes. Also, you smell real. I've wanted to sleep with you for a while."

"Oh . . . okay."

"But I also want to show you something."

"Do we order first?"

"Just pay for the wine."

~

"We should have ordered," says James.

"Yes. I'm famished."

It has been surprisingly good. James is not tentative in bed. Molly still feels like she can go again.

"Do you have anything in the kitchen?" he asks.

"I don't cook."

"I don't care. I cook. I can make a feast out of scraps. What do you have?"

"I might have half a potato or something. And corn-flakes. Butter, perhaps."

He sits up in bed. "That's pathetic."

The time is 0138 hours, they cannot order out. Molly brings two bowls of cornflakes with cold milk, which they devour on the bed.

Molly finishes first. She says, "James, I want you to measure me."

"What? Measure you how?"

"In every way, with every metric you know. Height, weight, arm circumference, blood, everything."

"Why?"

"I want to know if I'm human."

"Molly, what are you talking about?"

Molly starts talking. She does not tell him everything, just enough. Between her tale and his pointed questions, it takes the rest of the night.

~

James is not outwardly fazed by Molly's story. He becomes dispassionate and professional. He takes her to his lab and starts with the basics.

He hesitates. "If I take blood won't it . . . ?"

"The chemicals in the sample bottles seem to inactivate whatever it is. I tried it. Just don't use any plain tubes."

James takes the blood. "I'd like samples from a molly too. Tissue samples. For comparison. Do you have any prostheses?"

"No."

"Good. I want to do some whole-body scans."

"How long will this take?"

"A week. A month. Depends."

"Whatever shall we do while we're waiting?"

~

This is the first time Molly has felt happy since her parents died. In the daytime James experiments on Molly and the mollys—always talking about controls and calibration. At night they make love and eat food he cooks and discuss epigenetics and poetry.

Once, while they are sweating together, a molly appears in the doorway and joins them. It does not go bad while the three of them make love, and Molly kills it with regret and an ice pick the next morning.

"Has that happened before?" asks James. He does not help her dispose of the bodies.

"Not exactly," says Molly. "The mollys aren't all the same. Sometimes their personalities reflect my state of mind at the time. I don't know why, or what circumstances trigger that."

After this, James takes blood samples and biopsies at different times, depending on Molly's emotional state. He deliberately provokes her to anger, then tries to take a sample. This does not quite work out, because Molly punches him in the face.

He will not discuss even preliminary results. "It might affect further samples and change the outcome. I'll need to get a colleague to check my work when I'm done."

"But . . . this is private. I don't want other people knowing."

"I've already involved other people. I'm not Victor Frankenstein, Molly, I need the expertise of others. I'm not a radiographer, or a chemical pathologist. I need colleagues to interpret the data. They don't know what they're looking at, though."

Molly finds this unsettling, but she trusts James. She helps him stanch his bleeding nose.

~

Molly is unable to sleep, so she leaves James on the bed and does paperwork. She sees unopened letters, folders, bills, photos, and keepsakes from Southbourne Farm accusing her, so she begins work on them.

As Molly is finally getting to the end of the documents the lawyers left, she finds a dossier. It's discolored and all the paper is yellowed with oxidation. The pages are full of tight, typewritten text. Some of the *o*s and *p*s have solid windows. It's faded, but generally legible. She sits down on the floor to read.

A Letter to my Daughter

I knew you would find this. I meant for you to find it. You know about my past, a part of it, at any rate. You know that I did work abroad, and that I was an information gatherer and observer. There are other words for such as I was, like operative, agent, spy, but I find these melodramatic and inaccurate. Observer is the term I would choose, although I sometimes intervened.

They quickly embedded me in a country which accepted my Slavic looks, which boiled down to high cheekbones and grey eyes. They considered dyeing my hair blond, but I would not have it.

I had been in place for sixteen years. I did not know the details of my mission at first. My instructions were simple: blend in, become a local. Gain idiomatic proficiency with the language. Make friends. Take lovers. Become a citizen of this country. Attend university, a broad scatter of subjects, do not excel, do not stand out. Tick along, be vague, obfuscate when asked.

I did this. I cultivated friends who exemplified the folk people. I spent time with such people in their homes. They kiss visitors. I don't mean one or two. Every household member comes out and they kiss you one after the other. On the lips. It is beautiful.

The other people were less useful, by which I mean those who took on the attributes of our country. You see them, mimicking our fashions, our music, speaking our language in preference to their own. I could not learn from them other than to absorb a form of cultural inferiority complex.

We were taught to think of them as less than human, because of ideological differences, but they are just people. Like us. I reported back, told my handlers what I saw. This kind of feedback did not interest them. I had to talk about the locations of observatories and fuel stations. How many miles between such-

and-such petrol station and the nearest conurbation? What is the height of the grain silos in this other place? What are the main sources of protein? Take water samples from this river at points X, Y, and Z, three days apart. I did not understand, but ours is not to reason why.

Then there was a fallow period where I had no contact from the home country. I sank into my role and began to think of myself as the cover story, as this student going native. I may have fallen in love briefly. You remember love, right? That thing you said was tight friendship and a little fucking? I slipped, and did well on my exams, found myself in danger of graduating with honors. It is hard to play dumb.

I received instructions. I had forgotten that I even knew how to recognize the code. A student walked up to me and said the most cryptic thing. It took me a few moments to recall the required response. My handler had gone grey and sported a nice beer belly.

"Start loading your courses with biomedical science," he said. "Get good grades this time."

"Am I to become a doctor?" I asked.

"No, but take all the genetics courses you can find. Favor the professors with strong research profiles." He passed me a sheet. "Make sure these ones are on your list."

I did what he said and did not see him for two years. When I did see him, it was over clear spirits in a dismal basement. He handed me a photograph. It was one of my professors. "Get all the information you can about her most recent project." Then he let slip a curious thing that helped me understand my assignment. "It's getting late. Last week there was a twenty-four-hour period where no child was born in our country." He said nothing more, but seemed to drink a lot.

You probably live in a world where the fertility rates are so low that weeks without a child being born is a normal state of affairs. When I was young the total fertility rate was point-five per woman, and falling every year. If I've done a good job of schooling you, you should know what that means. Fertility rates worldwide plummeted, first in the developed nations, making scientists wonder if it was due to a modern toxin. They were on a hunt for it when it emerged that the same problems were shaking the developing world too. Bear in mind that some theorists believe the high fertility rate in some tropical zones was an adaptation to high infant mortality.

Anyway, nobody was having babies. The focus of my professor was not the cause, but the cure. I did not have access. I forwarded what I could, but I had taken enough classes to know it did not add up to anything.

My instructions came six weeks later. Steal it.

It sounds simple, but how do you steal an idea? Do you steal thoughts? Do you steal the realization of an idea?

I spent days deciding what I should steal, because this would be my final assignment. No going back afterward. They would know it was me. I mulled over my plan while one of my host families taught me how to make okroshka. Cooking is a great activity for when you need to get deep thinking done. I know it is the one skill I was unable to impart to you. I finalized my plan at the precise moment I measured out the dill.

After the household slept, I slipped out of the house, knowing I would never see it again. Entering the university was not hard, a student among other students studying or pretending to study. The laboratory was difficult, there were guards for a whole variety of reasons. There was some nuclear research done there, for example. I evaded them eventually. I knew my way around, could do it with my eyes closed. What I wanted was a vial, a sample. I brought an empty one with me. I would take a sample of the main fluid that was a distillation of the research, the embodiment, if not the thing itself. I drew it with a syringe and filled my vial. Then I got caught.

The laboratory lights came on and I became confused. The lab was secured by many identical unarmed women. I don't know for sure, but I was on the other side of the room, yards away, and there was enough time to inject myself with the fluid. It wouldn't matter if it was toxic—if they caught me I'd be dead anyway. Or I'd wish I were dead. The injection site hurt, but otherwise I felt okay. I don't remember this part well, but I fought my way out. The guards, the ones in the lab, they weren't well trained. Not like you, dorogoy!

I escaped alive enough to reach my contact. He was expecting a vial. He ended up having to extract me. I returned on a ship via merchant navy. Even from the dock I could see how much our country had changed, as you can imagine.

I felt overwhelmed and tired. I had broken ribs, a broken tooth that constantly bled into my mouth, blood in my urine, and a worrisome boggy mass on my left temple. I went to the nearest hospital, but when they asked my name, I would not or could not give the right one. I made one up on the spot. I sounded foreign, so it wasn't hard for them to accept me. The medical staff thought I was escaping domestic violence. I did not correct them.

When I left the hospital a few days later I did what you did: I got on a bus. I changed my appearance, came to live here.

I never saw my handlers. Either nobody looked, or they had more important things drawing their attention. I know my handler filed a report, and when I phoned the number I was supposed to, there was just a hiss. These people would have found me if they wanted to, Molly. They are serious people with serious motives. Committed.

Why did I tell you all this? Maybe the fluid I ingested has something to do with your condition.

One last thing: I sometimes suspect that they are watching us. By "they" I mean the people I used to work for. I see people who seem to be working too hard not to look at me, a little too casual, a little too uninterested. I think they come onto the farm sometimes. If you ever run into a problem you can't deal with, the number on your arm will sort it out. It's a private security firm who have the utmost discretion and have been briefed on your condition. It's all paid for.

I love you with everything I have, Molly, though I do not have much left.

Do svidaniya.

There is no signature, but Molly knows it is not fake. She even imagines she can smell her mother's perfume on the paper. Most important, the letter reads like Ma spoke. A lot of the background information Molly already suspected, but this is her first hint that the mollys might be artificial, instead of some natural aberration or mutation.

Was I meant to populate the world with mollys to save the human race from extinction? That's an absurd solution.

She does not know how to feel, and she is surprised when a heavy teardrop falls onto the paper.

⁓

Molly debates with herself whether to tell James about her mother's history lesson. Her mind churns as she drives home after a busy day. She has not heard from James all day, but when she unlocks the front door he is waiting for her.

"Hi!" says Molly.

James nods. "You should sit down."

"What's wrong?" She sees the large plastic folder beside him. "Oh."

James rubs his eyes. "Just sit down, Molly. Please. I . . . sit down."

She sits opposite him, on the floor, legs tucked under

her. Not an affectation; she does not trust herself to resist lashing out.

"I found Leon."

"I wasn't looking for him," says Molly.

James hands her a photograph. It shows a mess, a round excavation bounded by four detached limbs, and a head that might have been Leon's.

"What happened to him?"

"You did."

"You mean a molly . . . ?"

"No. You passed something on to him, something that grew out of him eventually." James gives her another photograph. This time it's an abdominal scan showing an irregular mass.

"Leon had a tumor?"

"That's not him. That's me."

She reaches for his arm, but he withdraws.

"I'm sorry. We can find a way to—"

"You did this, Molly."

"What are you talking about?"

"When I tested you I found foreign cells and a slightly enlarged spleen. The mollys don't have those cells. Almost as a lark, I tested my own blood. I found the same foreign cells. I scanned myself and found the mass. And it's growing rapidly. This is what killed Leon. It's a slow-growing molly."

"Wait. It can't . . . I—"

He stands and drops the rest of the documents in front of her. "You've killed me."

He leaves, and she does not try to follow.

~

Molly understands. Whatever else she is, she is now a weapon. She deals death no matter what, even when she does not know it. James will not, cannot, face it with her. She thinks she might have grown to love him and, perversely, is glad he made this decision. He would have been killed by a molly sooner or later. Like her parents. She takes the package downstairs, to the basement. She fires up the furnace, opens the door, and throws all the research inside. She watches it burn, feels the heat on her face, and coldly decides what comes next.

~

Her resignation from the university is handwritten. She does not need to, but closure is important. A part of her wishes she would bump into James while clearing out her desk, but it does not happen. She is too scared to ask after him, unwilling to deal with the guilt if he's dead.

She then takes a week to build her dungeon. She has

metal rings on the walls and floor, along with chains, handcuffs, and plastic ties. She piles all the furniture in the middle of the front room. She has cans and cans of lighter fluid.

Molly pricks herself with her hunting knife and sprinkles blood into the middle of the furniture.

Then she sits and waits.

Four

I am trying to stretch my arms and legs as far as I can while she comes to the end of her tale. I ache from immobility.

"All my life I thought the mollys were holding me back, but it wasn't them. It was me all along." Molly takes a sip of water. "You don't have to believe my story, but you do have to remember."

She stops talking, swallows the last of the water, and sets the glass down. The knocking on the door is as loud as thunderclaps. The door shakes in the hinges, like loose teeth.

"I'm a molly," I say.

"Yes," Molly Southbourne says.

"Why don't I feel like killing you?"

"I don't know. You guys don't all behave the same. You're the eleventh one I've tied up and tried to reason with like this. It didn't end well for the other ten."

I swallow. "So, what now? Do we fight?"

"We've already done that. That's why I'm over here and you're in chains."

The tattoo itches. "What, then?"

"Have you ever read Roshodan? Of course you haven't. You haven't read anything. Well, my mother made me read his monographs. He said, 'With each failure, each insult, each wound to the psyche, we are created anew. This new self is who we must battle each day or face extinction of the spirit.' I think I'm the embodiment of that sentiment."

I say nothing. The memory of that treatise surges to the surface, and I know the rest of the quotation. *But is extinction such a terrible thing? Each mistake, when examined, can lead to positive change, to a stronger mind. Only by subordinating pride can we elevate the spirit.* Is she going to make me extinct?

Play dumb. "What does that mean?"

"Nothing. You are free." She gets up. "I'm tired. *For sleep is good, but Death is better still—The best is never to be born at all.* It's up to you now. If you want, you can be Molly Southbourne, or you can assume a different name and let her never have been born. I do not care. I'm done with it."

Molly Southbourne throws me a set of keys, then strikes a match and drops it to the floor. Flame bursts up, then rushes toward the door and under it. There are screeches from the other side, and the hammering stops. She sighs, then stands. She takes one last look at me, then opens the door. I can hear screaming just before she slams the door shut after her. Over the crackle of the flames I hear the sounds of hand-to-hand combat. I can imagine each move, each strike, as if it's me in the fight. It *is* me in the fight, on both sides. I might have stayed mesmerized, except for the acrid miasma I have to breathe. I unlock myself, go for the second door, which opens to a short flight of stairs, and I try to get out of the front door, but it has been sealed with nails. I go upstairs, break a window, cover the jagged edge with a curtain, and slip out onto a shelf, and from there, I hang by my hands, then let go. It's a hard, painful landing, but no injuries. No new ones, at any rate.

I limp away from the house and see that smoke is starting to rise from the windows, dark wisps against the dawn light. There is a phone box just at the end of the street. I call the number on my new tattoo after reversing the charges.

"Name?" says a voice.

"Molly Southbourne," I say.

About the Author

Photograph by Carla Roadnight

TADE THOMPSON lives and works in the south of England. His background is in medicine, psychiatry, and social anthropology. His first novel, *Making Wolf,* won the Golden Tentacle Award at the 2016 Kitschies. His second novel, *Rosewater,* is on the 2016 Locus Recommended Reading List, and his short story "The Apologists" has been shortlisted for a British Science Fiction Association Award. He enjoys jazz, comics, and baking deformed bread.

TOR·COM

Science fiction. Fantasy. The universe. And related subjects.

*

More than just a publisher's website, *Tor.com* is a venue for **original fiction, comics,** and **discussion** of the entire field of SF and fantasy, in all media and from all sources. Visit our site today—and join the conversation yourself.